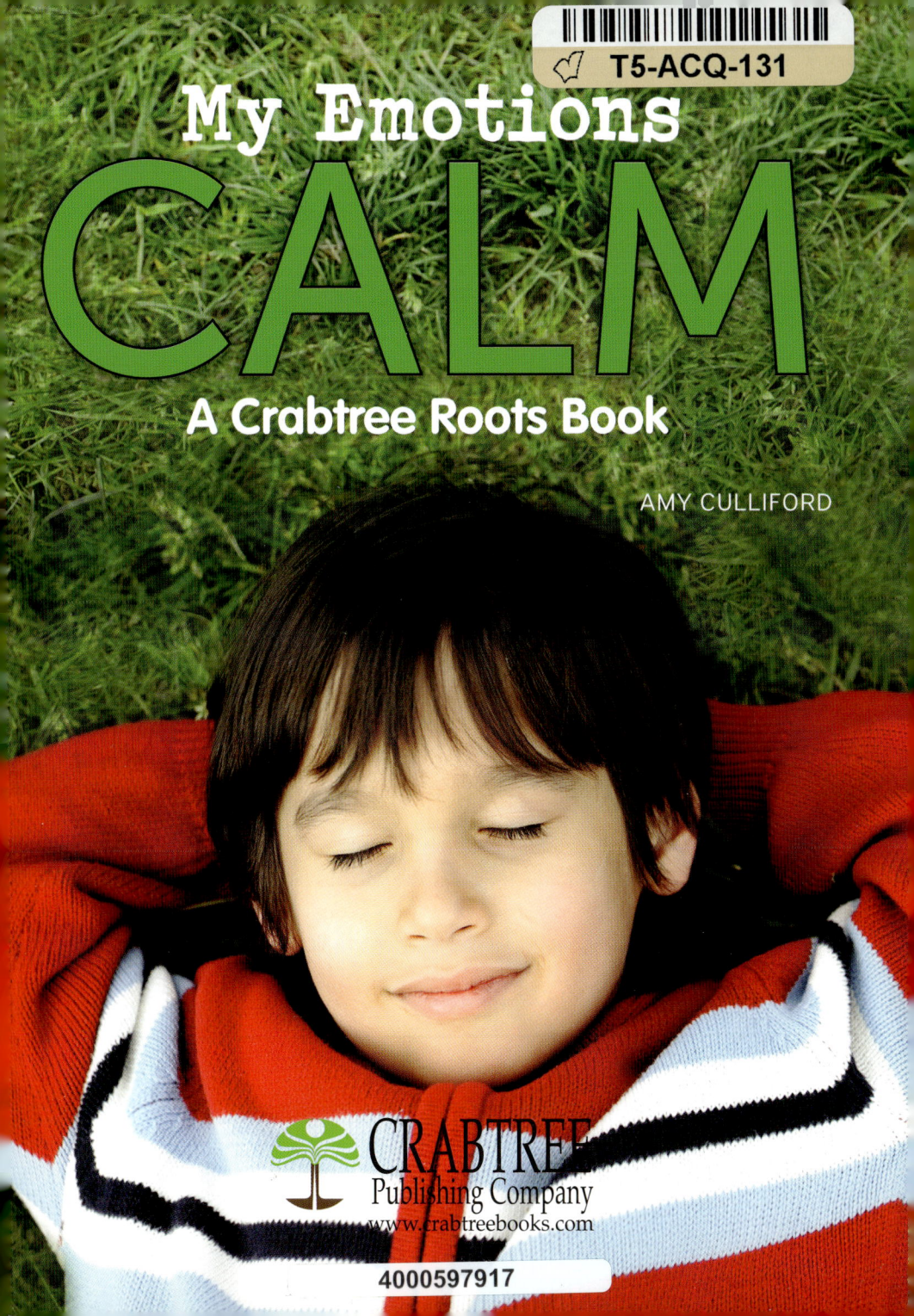

My Emotions
CALM

A Crabtree Roots Book

AMY CULLIFORD

School-to-Home Support for Caregivers and Teachers

This book helps children grow by letting them practice reading. Here are a few guiding questions to help the reader with building his or her comprehension skills. Possible answers appear here in red.

Before Reading:
- What do I think this book is about?
    - *This book is about how to feel calm.*
    - *This book is about what feeling calm looks or feels like.*
- What do I want to learn about this topic?
    - *I want to learn what makes people feel calm.*
    - *I want to learn what feeling calm looks like.*

During Reading:
- I wonder why...
    - *I wonder why we smile when we are calm.*
    - *I wonder why baths make people calm.*

- What have I learned so far?
    - *I have learned that drawing can make you feel calm.*
    - *I have learned that people sit when they are calm.*

After Reading:
- What details did I learn about this topic?
    - *I have learned that there are many ways you can feel calm.*
    - *I have learned that you can think things through when you are calm.*
- Read the book again and look for the vocabulary words.
    - *I see the word **drawing** on page 4 and the word **music** on page 8. The other vocabulary words are found on page 14.*

What makes you **calm**?

Drawing makes me calm.

I sit when I am calm.

7

Music makes me calm.

I can think when I am calm.

A **bath** makes me calm.

I **smile** when I am calm.

What makes you calm?

Word List
Sight Words

a	I	when
am	makes	you
can	what	

Words to Know

bath   **calm**   **drawing**

music   **smile**

40 Words

What makes you **calm**?

Drawing makes me calm.

I sit when I am calm.

Music makes me calm.

I can think when I am calm.

A **bath** makes me calm.

I **smile** when I am calm.

What makes you calm?

Written by: Amy Culliford
Designed by: Rhea Wallace
Series Development: James Earley
Proofreader: Ellen Rodger
Educational Consultant: Marie Lemke M.Ed.

Photographs:
Shutterstock: Juan Pablo Gonzaález: cover; ZouZou: p. 1;
ESB Professional: p. 3, 14; LightField Studio: p. 5, 14; Africa Studio: p. 8, 14; Newman Studio: p. 9, 14; Chz_mhOng: p. 10, 14; narikan: p. 11, 14; Rusian Shugushev: p. 13

My Emotions
CALM

Library and Archives Canada Cataloguing in Publication

Title: Calm / Amy Culliford.
Names: Culliford, Amy, 1992- author.
Description: Series statement: My emotions | "A Crabtree roots book".
Identifiers: Canadiana (print) 20210156635 | Canadiana (ebook) 20210156643 | ISBN 9781427139641 (hardcover) | ISBN 9781427139702 (softcover) | ISBN 9781427133397 (HTML) | ISBN 9781427139764 (read-along ebook) | ISBN 9781427133991 (EPUB)
Subjects: LCSH: Calmness—Juvenile literature.
Classification: LCC BF575.C35 C85 2021 | DDC j152.4—dc23

Library of Congress Cataloging-in-Publication Data

Names: Culliford, Amy, 1992- author.
Title: Calm / Amy Culliford.
Description: New York : Crabtree Publishing, 2021. | Series: My emotions, a crabtree roots book | Includes index.
Identifiers: LCCN 2021009520 (print) | LCCN 2021009521 (ebook) | ISBN 9781427139641 (hardcover) | ISBN 9781427139702 (paperback) | ISBN 9781427139764 (read along) | ISBN 9781427133397 (ebook) | ISBN 9781427133991 (epub)
Subjects: LCSH: Calmness--Juvenile literature. | Emotions in children--Juvenile literature.
Classification: LCC BF575.C35 C85 2021 (print) | LCC BF575. C35 (ebook) | DDC 155.4/124--dc23
LC record available at https://lccn.loc.gov/2021009520
LC ebook record available at https://lccn.loc.gov/2021009521

Crabtree Publishing Company
www.crabtreebooks.com   1-800-387-7650

Printed in the U.S.A./062021/CG20210401

Copyright © 2022 **CRABTREE PUBLISHING COMPANY**

All rights reserved. No part of this publication may be reproduced, stored in a retrieval system or be transmitted in any form or by any means, electronic, mechanical, photocopying, recording, or otherwise, without the prior written permission of Crabtree Publishing Company. In Canada: We acknowledge the financial support of the Government of Canada through the Canada Book Fund for our publishing activities.

Published in the United States
Crabtree Publishing
347 Fifth Avenue, Suite 1402-145
New York, NY, 10016

Published in Canada
Crabtree Publishing
616 Welland Ave.
St. Catharines, Ontario L2M 5V6